carol duffy

The CHANGING

# Princess' Blankets

paintings by
catherine hyde

templar publishing

the

✻ the bright sun    ✻ every dres

✻ the princess stayed

✻ the ocean's blanket    ✻ the forest'

✻ the earth's blanket    ✻ the terribl

✻ the wonderful music

✻ the roaring, glittering sea    ✻ the stranger

✻ under a blanke

*paintings*

aker in the land

hivering     ❋nearing dusk

lanket     ❋the mountain's blanket

magic     ❋one evening

❋they saw their souls

was not heard of again

f stars

*the bright sun*

# A princess lived, once, who was always cold.

Even when the bright sun was at its warmest she refused to get out of her bed.

Her father, the King, ordered huge, roaring fires to be lit in every room of the

palace but, although this made the royal servants so hot that the sweat dripped

from the ends of their noses and splashed onto the marble floors, the Princess

remained cold. Her mother, the Queen, instructed that the Princess was always to

be dressed in the heaviest fleeces and the warmest woollens but, despite the fact

that every dressmaker in the land stitched and sewed far into the night, and whole

flocks of sheep shivered fleeceless out in their fields, the Princess stayed cold.

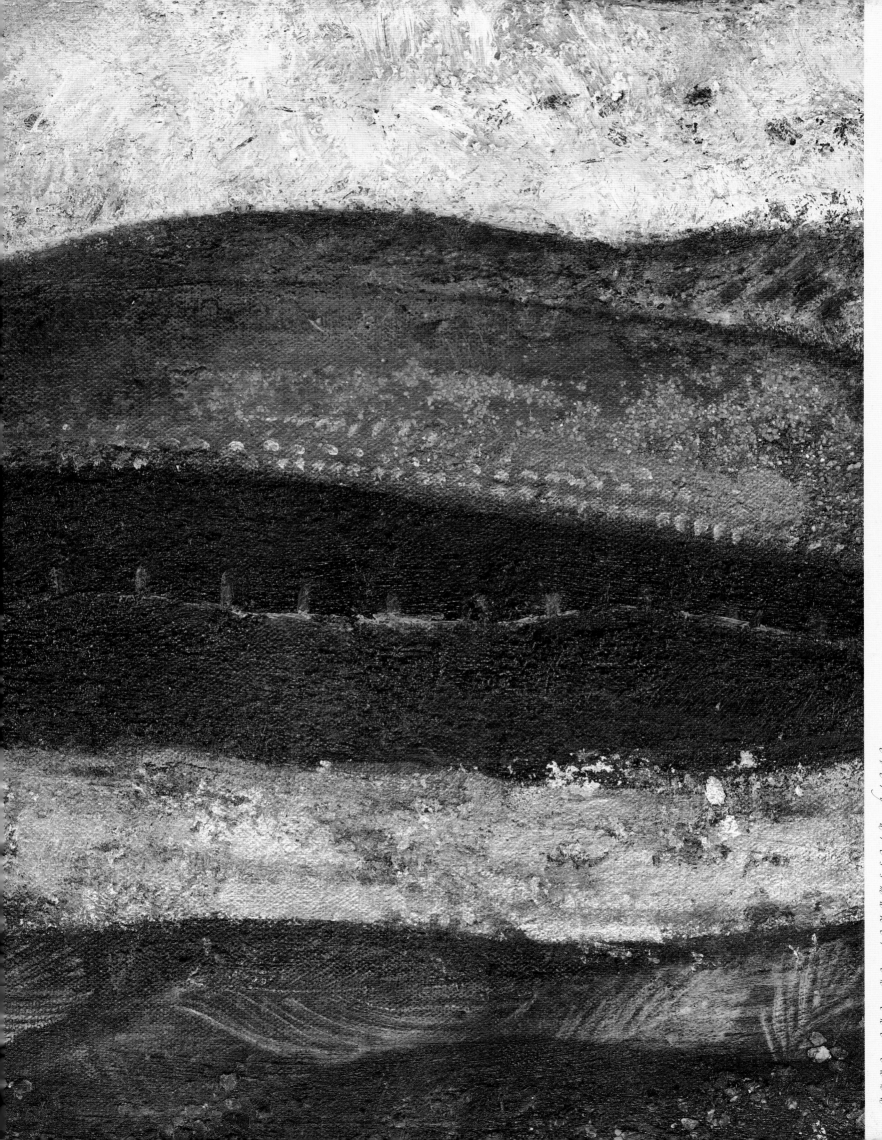

every dressmaker in the land

One day, the King announced that anyone in the land who could think of a way to stop the Princess feeling so cold would be rewarded in any manner they chose, even unto half his kingdom.

People came from far and wide, carrying hot-water bottles plump with boiling water, or bearing bright copper warming pans crammed with glowing coals; bringing nightcaps, nightgowns, thermal underwear, bed socks and sleeping gloves. Families emptied their drawers and chests of bed linen and blankets and made their way hopefully up to the palace. But it was all useless. The Princess stayed shivering in her bed, dressed from head to toe in wool and fleeces, shawled, gloved, hatted and scarfed, complaining of the cold.

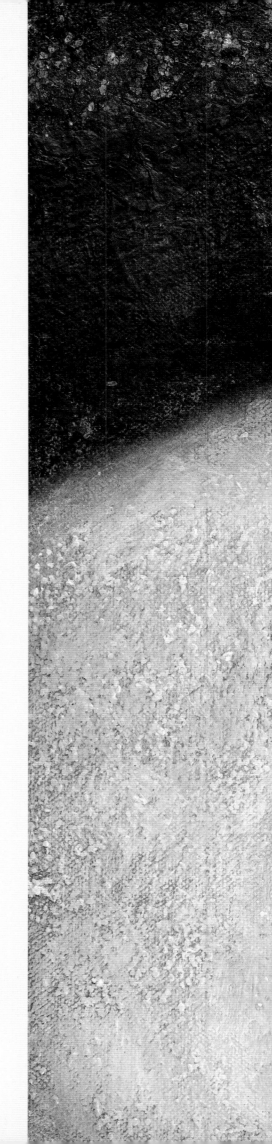

*the princess stayed shivering*

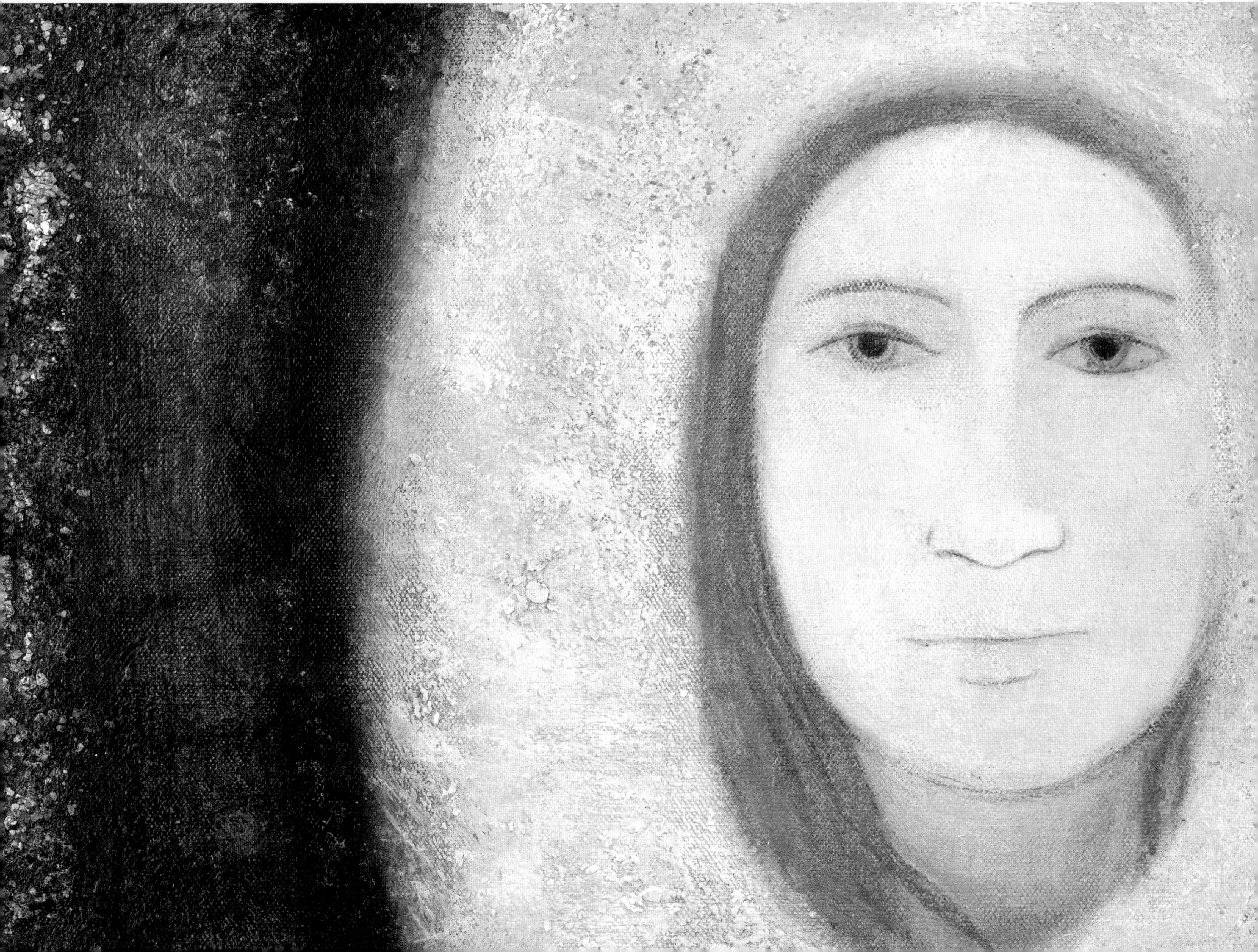

It was nearing dusk one evening, when a

stranger arrived at the palace demanding to

see the King. The man was dressed in black

clothes and did not bow when the King

entered. He had hard, grey eyes like polished

stones. He explained to the King that he knew

magic and could stop the Princess suffering

from the cold. If he was successful, as he was

certain he would be, he planned to carry the

Princess back to his own land to be his wife.

When the Queen heard that the stranger

was planning to take the Princess away,

should he earn his reward, she was unhappy

and remonstrated with the King. She was

sure her daughter would not care to be the

wife of a man with such stony eyes. But the

King said no, the stranger should have his

chance, and it would be the price the

Princess would have to pay to find warmth.

The stranger was escorted to the Princess' bedchamber and stood before her. The Princess was sitting

up in bed, wrapped in a fleece. The man told her why he was there and that soon he hoped to win

her for his wife. The Princess felt afraid, for the stranger had cruel eyes, and even though she longed

to feel warm, she hoped that he would not be the person who would cure her.

"How cold do you feel?" asked the stranger.

I shall make it difficult for this arrogant man, thought the Princess to herself. So she answered,

"As cold as the ocean is."

The stranger gave a small smile, and turned on his heel. He was gone for some time and,

although the Princess was freezing, she was glad to think she had got rid of the proud man. But no

sooner had she thought this than he appeared again in her room. He flung down a huge blanket onto

her bed. The Princess gasped as the blanket swamped her. It was woven in blues and greens and

greys, and it moved over her body in clumsy, urgent waves. It smelled salty and seaweedy as she

tossed her head on the pillow, and when she looked closer at the pattern on the blanket, she saw that

many fish swam in it and that dolphins leaped in its borders. There were whales in the blanket and sad,

sunken ships. There were octopuses and jellyfish. The blanket lapped at her, and she felt sick.

"THE OCEAN'S BLANKET," he said.

overleaf: *the ocean's blanket*

"Warmer now?" demanded the stranger.

But the Princess was even colder than before, and trembled in her bed.

I will not go with you, she thought. So she replied,

"No. I am as cold as the forest is."

The man nodded at her, and left the room. The Princess lay in her bed, hoping that she had seen the

last of him, but soon enough she heard his footsteps at her door. He came into the bedchamber and

tossed a huge blanket over her.

The blanket was coarse and spiky and, as the Princess tried to push it off, it scratched at her arms

and hands, drawing blood. It was roughly woven in blacks and browns and dark greens. The blanket

smelled mossy and damp, and the Princess saw that it was patterned with ancient trees and birds of

prey, embroidered with dark undergrowth and small, wild creatures.

"THE FOREST'S BLANKET," he said.

overleaf: *the forest's blanket*

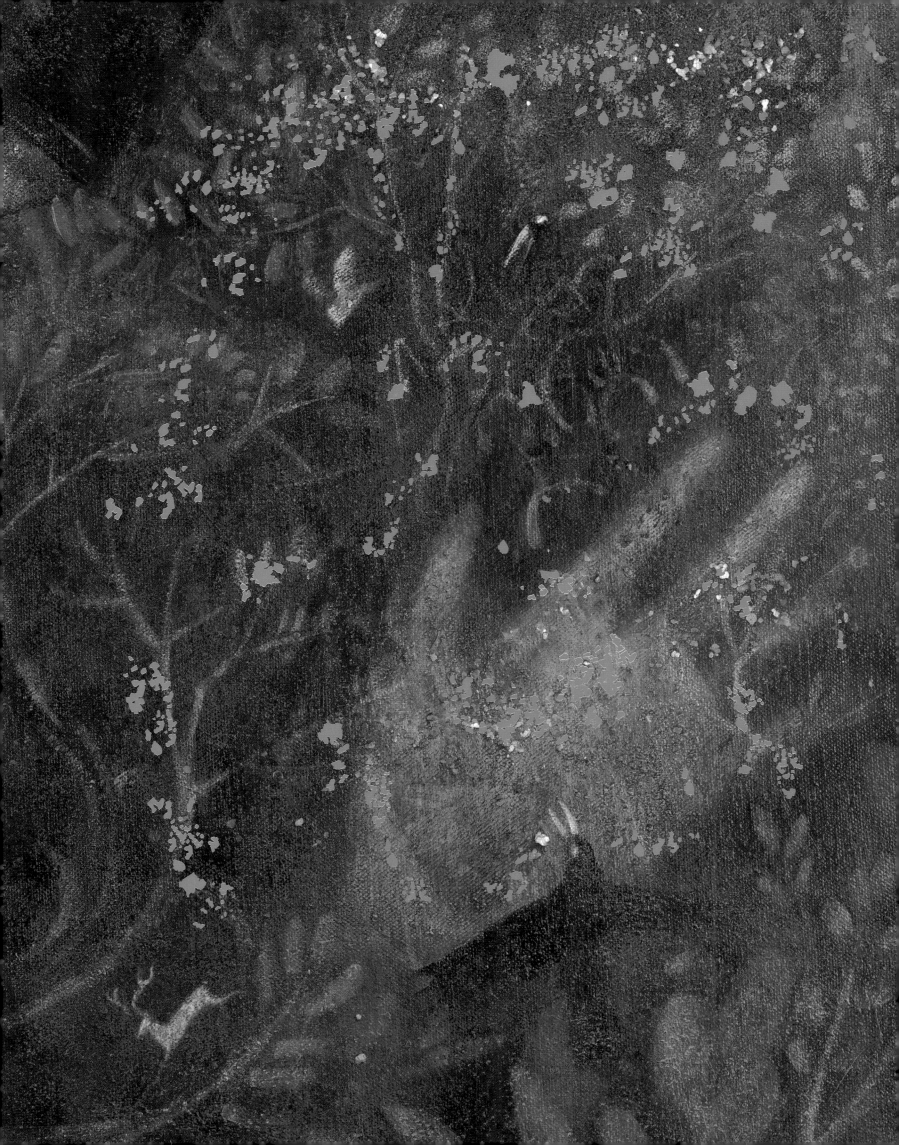

There was darkness in the blanket; there were frightening shadows. There were brambles and snakes.

The blanket clawed at her and she felt faint.

"Warmer now?" asked the stranger.

But she was colder than ever and her teeth were chattering.

You will not win me, thought the Princess. Then she replied,

"No. I am as cold as the mountain is."

The man looked angry, but he turned and strode from the room. He was gone for quite a while, and

the Princess began to hope that he would not return. But the hope froze in her heart as she saw the

stranger enter her bedchamber yet again. He threw a great blanket over her bed. The blanket was so

heavy that the Princess could hardly breathe as it pressed down on her. It was woven in many different

greys, and shot through with sparkling silver. She pushed against it with her hands, but it was as hard

as stone and as jagged as rock, and her fine nails broke against it. She looked down and saw the

pattern of sheer cliffs and glaciers. There were ice-cold streams in the blanket and dark ravines.

Frozen snow was heaped in its borders. The blanket bore down on her and she felt dizzy.

"THE MOUNTAIN'S BLANKET," he said.

overleaf: *the mountain's blanket*

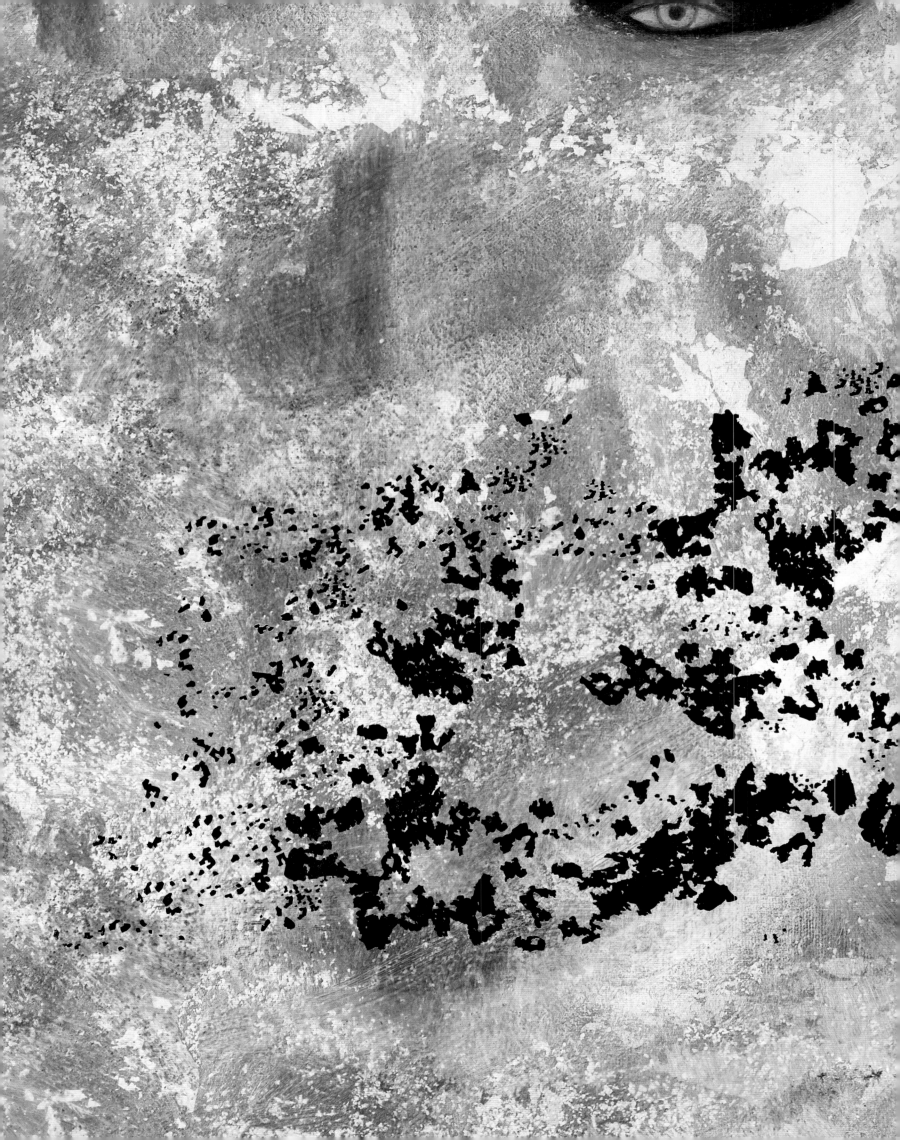

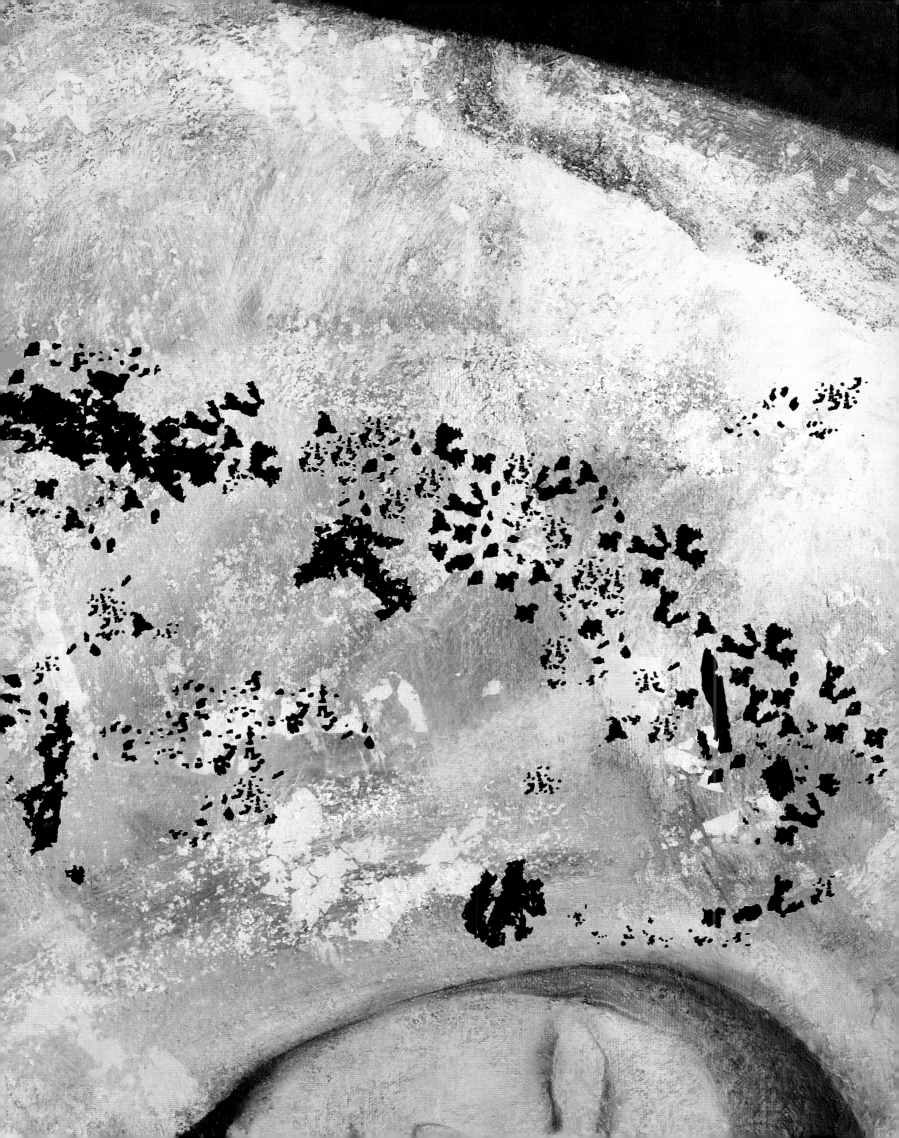

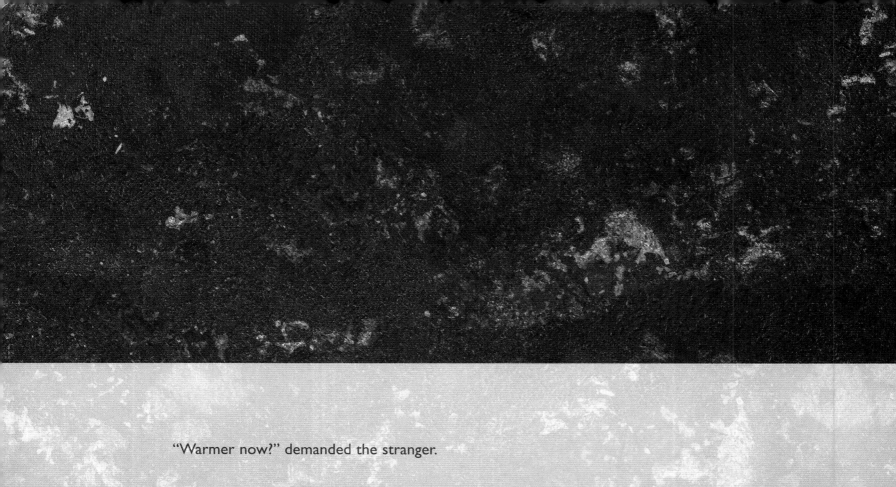

"Warmer now?" demanded the stranger.

But the Princess was like ice, and chittered on her bed.

I will not be yours, she thought.  So she said,

"No.  I am as cold as the earth."

The stranger stared at her, then walked from the room.  A long time passed, and the Princess prayed

that he was gone for good.  But as the prayer formed on her pale lips, the man stood before her once

more.  He held a huge blanket in his arms, and spread it over her.

The Princess moaned as the blanket came down over her, covering even her face. It smelled of dead

leaves and decay, and felt moist and clammy. She pulled it from her face, feeling its soft, crumbly texture

in her hands. The blanket was woven in the darkest brown. It was patterned with worms and spiders,

and embroidered with corms and bulbs. There were tangled roots in the blanket, pale, hollow skulls,

and the crumbling bones of dead creatures. The blanket clung to her like a shroud, and she felt weak.

"THE EARTH'S BLANKET," he said.

overleaf: *the earth's blanket*

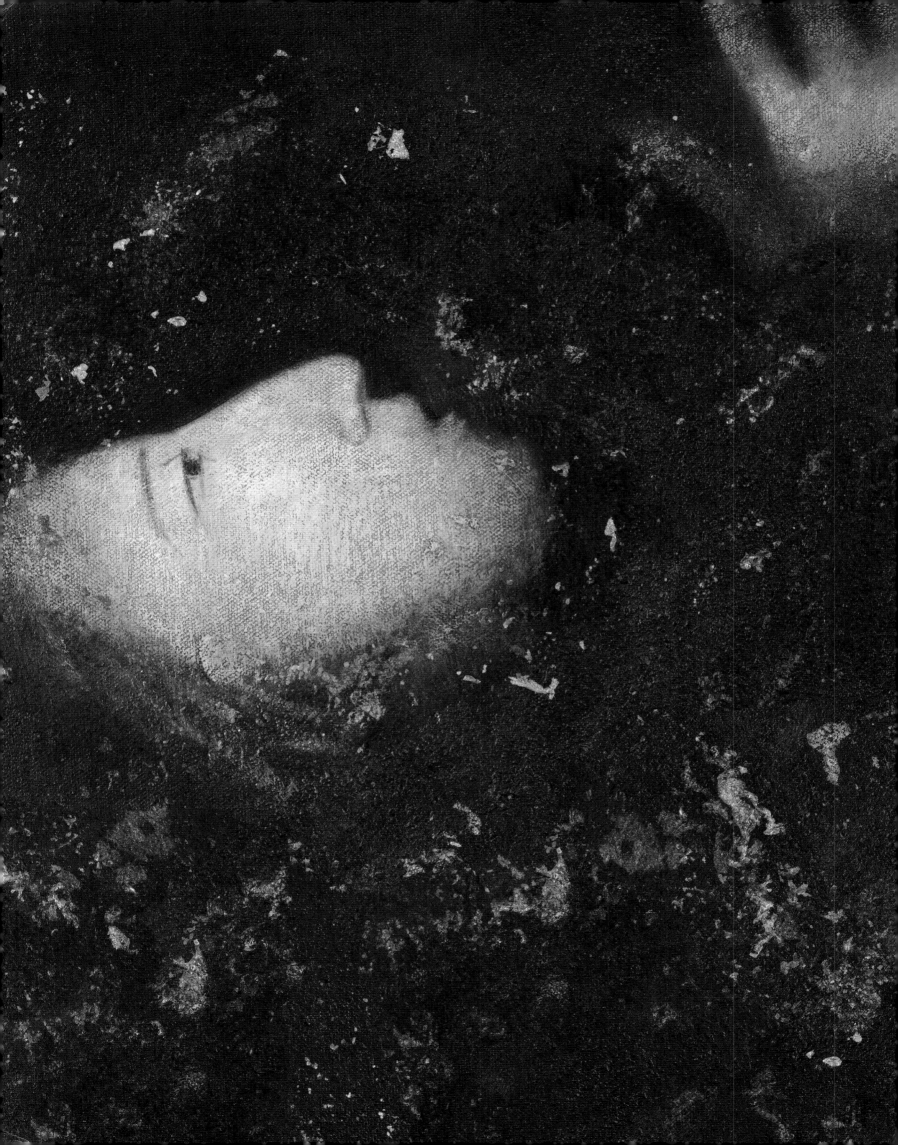

"Warmer now?" asked the man.

There was no reply.

"How cold?" demanded the stranger.

"How cold now?"

But the Princess was too cold to answer him, and

the furious man had no choice but to leave the

bedchamber, and to kick his heels in the palace

corridor until there was further news.

And now the people were sad and frightened,

because there was no ocean to fish in. The ocean

was one of the Princess' blankets, and all the empty

fishing boats lay uselessly on the sands and mud

flats, and folk went hungry for fish. Nor was there

any longer a forest to pick fruit from, or hunt in,

or to chop and gather wood from to make fire.

The forest was one of the Princess' blankets, and

there were no trees left and no birds to sing in

them. And the mountain was gone. The mountain

was one of the Princess' blankets, so there were

no high peaks to collect rain from the clouds and

no mountain streams bringing fresh water tumbling

down to the towns and villages. There was no

earth. The earth was one of the Princess' blankets,

so there were no vegetables growing in the soil,

no corn or wheat swaying in the breeze, no

colourful flowers or cool green grass. And if

somebody died, their poor loved ones had

nowhere to bury them. Word passed from mouth

to mouth that all this had come about because the

Princess would not love the man with stony eyes.

One evening, in late summer, a musician was walking quite near to the palace, doodling on his flute. He was new to the country and wondered why the land was so bleak and arid, and why the people were so gloomy. He stopped for a while at an inn, and came to hear about the cold Princess. He heard about the terrible magic done by the stranger and how none of it had made the Princess warm. The musician had a kind and good heart, and he made up his mind to go to the palace himself to see if he could help. He bowed before the sad King, and kissed the hand of the tearful Queen, and then he was led into the bedchamber, where the cold Princess lay beneath her blankets of ocean and forest and mountain and earth.

As soon as he looked at her and saw how beautiful she was, and how cold, the musician's heart flooded with love and he was lost. He took out his flute and began to play the loveliest tune he knew, playing with his soul so that she would know how much he loved her. After a little while, the Princess turned her head on the pillow and looked towards him. The musician played on, until the Princess sat up a little, listening intently to the wonderful music. She pulled her shawls tightly around her shoulders. When he had played the last note of his melody, the musician put down his flute and knelt by the side of the Princess' bed. He took her cold hands from where they lay on the blanket and kissed each one with his warm lips, fingertip by fingertip. As he did so, the Princess felt his warmth flood into her fingers, so that their skin burned with a surge of life and energy. She reached up and touched his hair with her tingling hands. As she did so, the earth's blanket slipped from the bed. Then the musician bent down and kissed the Princess' pale cheeks and the Princess flushed as she felt his warm breath on her face. She put her arms about the musician's neck to hide her blushes, and the mountain's blanket slid to the floor.

The musician heard the Princess sigh in his ear and thought he would die with love, but he

took her face in his hands and kissed her eyelids. Two warm tears trickled down the Princess'

face, and the forest's blanket slipped from the bed. The musician and the Princess looked into

each other's eyes and they saw their souls there, and, when the musician kissed her on the lips,

the Princess' heart warmed her whole body with love. The ocean's blanket lay on the floor.

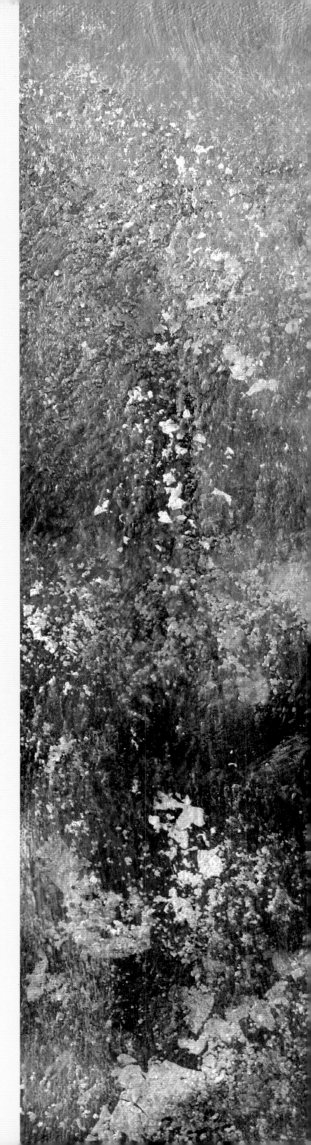

Outside, the roaring, glittering sea rushed in foaming,

white waves for the shore, and the shouting, pointing

fishermen ran to their boats.  The forest shook the

birds from its hair, tossing its leaves and branches in

the wind, shadowy and dark at the edge of the town.

Further still, the huge mountain towered against the

skyline, its snowy peaks covered in cloud, as though it

was deep in thought.  Later, as evening began to fall, the

fertile earth grew blurred and soft, nurturing the growing

harvest, nourishing its scented flowers, nursing its dead.

the roaring, glittering sea

The people went back to their ordinary lives, grateful

for the earth and the ocean, for the forest and the

mountain. The stranger was not heard of again,

although from time to time there were rumours that

he had drowned, or had fallen from a great height; that

he had been crushed by a tree, or been buried alive.

The King, with the Queen beside him, kept his word

and told the musician to name his reward, even unto

half the kingdom. The musician asked to stay always

by the Princess' side, and the Princess agreed.

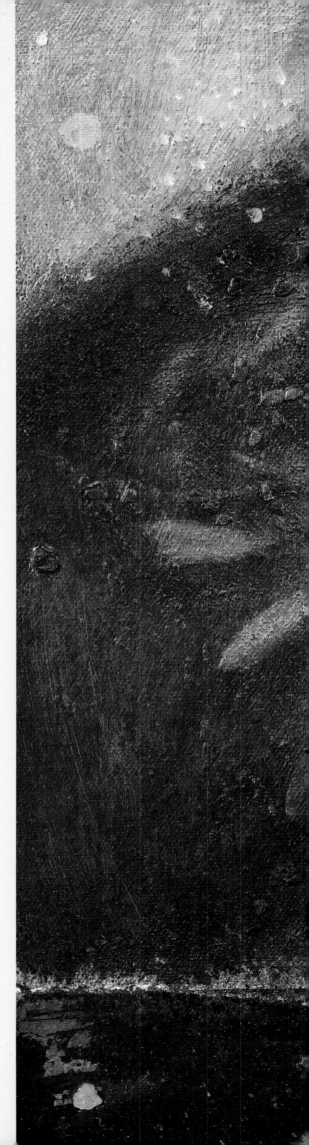

the stranger was not heard of again

*Sometimes,*

on summer nights, they slept outside, hearing

the mountain stream, and the sea, and the wind

in the trees, under a blanket of stars.

under a blanket of stars

*For Vivien* – C.A.D.

*For my parents,
John and Marina,
with my love* – C.H.

*carol ann duffy* is one of today's most highly esteemed poets, playwrights and writers. Described by *The Guardian* as "the most popular living poet in Britain", her work is widely studied on the English Literature syllabus in schools and has won numerous prestigious awards and prizes. Carol Ann has been awarded both an OBE and a CBE and is a Fellow of the Royal Society of Literature. She lives in Manchester with her daughter, Ella.

*catherine hyde* trained in Fine Art at Central Saint Martins College of Art and Design in London, and has since become a highly successful artist, holding exhibitions at galleries nationwide. This is the first time she has interpreted a text as a series of paintings, and she says of *The Princess' Blankets*, "I read and reread the story many times until I saw it in terms of atmosphere and colour. I wanted the mood to change like the seasons as the story progressed, so the paintings run from hot and bright to moody and harsh and finally to warm and sensual." Catherine lives with her husband and two teenage daughters in Cornwall.

## A TEMPLAR BOOK

First published in the UK in 2008 by Templar Publishing, an imprint of The Templar Company plc,
The Granary, North Street, Dorking, Surrey, RH4 1DN, UK
www.templarco.co.uk

Illustration copyright © 2008 by Catherine Hyde • Text copyright © 2008 by Carol Ann Duffy
Design copyright © 2008 by The Templar Company plc

First edition

ISBN 978-1-84011-201-6 (hardback edition)
ISBN 978-1-84011-173-6 (limited edition in slipcase) • ISBN 978-1-84011-339-6 (softback edition)

Designed by janie louise hunt • Edited by Stella Gurney
Printed in China

*In memory of
the Solomon Browne*

*For LB with love* – j.l.h.